Wheel of Danger

The last week of term seemed to drag for Mike Baxter and his friends Sandra, Ranji and Andy. They wouldn't be seeing each other till Saturday, when they planned to make their first big expedition out to the disused mill Sandra had discovered on the moors. It didn't seem as though anyone had bothered with it for donkey's years and the children were determined to get the water wheel turning again.

"We'll have that wheel going round before we go back to school, even if it kills us," said Sandra. The others had laughed, but later on, they had reason to remember those words.

Wheel of Danger

ROBERT LEESON

Illustrated by Anthony Kerins

Young Lions

First published in Great Britain 1986
by William Collins Sons & Co. Ltd
First published in Young Lions 1987
8 Grafton Street, London W1X 3LA

Young Lions is an imprint
of the Collins Publishing Group

Text © 1986 Robert Leeson
Illustrations © 1986 Anthony Kerins

Printed in Great Britain by
William Collins Sons & Co. Ltd, Glasgow

Contents

For Ben

Mike Baxter says:
   When they make you feel small –
         you're small

   When they make your parents feel small –
         you vanish

1

Our Gang in Trouble

I had it all worked out. I was going to get my new mate Steven out of Spotty Sam's gang at school, and into ours. I planned a big ceremony. One Saturday morning, I'd take Steve through the park to our oak tree. It's a funny old tree, centuries old, and it grows sideways out of a big grass bank.

All our gang would be waiting, sitting along the main branch. There'd be Ranji, then Sandra – she's the oldest – and her fat little brother Andy. Except that he isn't little any more. He's a lot bigger. But he's still fat.

Then Steven would swear an oath of loyalty. He's very good at swearing, is Steve. Then we'd break a bottle of champagne over his head and he'd get his seat on the oak branch. We all had our own place and that's where we sit when we have our planning sessions on Saturday.

I didn't rush things. For one, Sandra thought

Steven's brother, Spotty Sam, was a gorilla and thick as two planks. So he is, but I reckoned Steve was OK. But Ranji didn't really trust anyone who'd been in Spotty Sam's mob. So, it had to hang about. I let it ride over Christmas and waited for the good weather to come.

But I waited too long. In the New Year, things started to come unstuck. First of all, Ranji left. His Dad lost his job. The mill shut down. They were closing mills left, right and centre. The buildings stood all empty with their windows smashed, waiting for the scrappies to come and take the machines out and the demo men to bring the old ball and chain and break the walls up. Ranji's family moved out to another town.

Then Sandra started going funny. Well, she took up jogging. You could see her running round the park in the mornings with Andy puffing and blowing behind her, red in the face. Then she started *harrying*. You know, long distance running, for competitions. And at weekends she disappeared, with the Harrier Club, running out over the moors to Penfold Forest and places like that, miles away. Andy reckoned she fancied the bloke that ran the club. But he didn't say that when she was around. He's not so green as he's cabbage looking, our Andy.

So, instead of getting bigger, our gang was starting to break up. Some Saturdays there was no one around the old oak tree at all. It was depressing.

Spring came. The weather got warmer. It looked as though we'd have a great summer. Things ought to get better, I told myself.

But they didn't.

2

Andy, the Menace

As summer came on, things got worse. With Ranji gone, and Sandra busy with her hairy-legged harriers, Andy started hanging around me. I felt sorry for him in a way. They've no Mum and their Dad's working all hours and weekends as well.

But then, he started coming round to our house, while I was still having my Saturday morning kip. Then our Mum'd wake me up. That was bad enough.

She'd shout up the stairs: 'Andy's called round for you.' It's a wonder she didn't say: 'Andy wants you to come out and play.' I mean, how can you explain to people? I was in the second year at school and Andy was still in the juniors, even if he did look like a mini-elephant.

There he'd be, waiting, with his stunt bike and his crash helmet on. Clumsy Colin was nothing in it. What could I do? I couldn't pretend I was going

10

somewhere else, could I? Being rotten ought to be easy. But it isn't.

So I trundled off with Andy down to the shelters. It's a big piece of waste ground where they used to have air-raid shelters during the War. It's rough and bumpy with bushes and thick grass with trails up and down where kids ride their bikes. As soon as we arrived, there was a crowd of juniors waiting to have a go on Andy's iron. It was bigger and better than anyone else's. His Dad doesn't pay much attention to him – that's all left to Sandra – but he forks out for things like that.

The way Andy showed off was sickening. He'd shove all the smaller kids away, then shout:

'Get off. My mate Mike's having the first go.'

I didn't know where to put myself. My mate Mike!

What made it worse was, the first go I had on the bike, I came off. I was flying up this slope, getting ready to take off when I hit the top. But I jerked too hard on the bars and the flipping machine somersaulted, with me still on it.

'Hey, great stuff, Mike!' shouted Andy. I gave him back the bike, and vanished. But Andy didn't seem to notice. He was too busy giving orders to that mob of kids.

I sloped off across the waste ground. Then I found I couldn't get out that way. They'd fenced off a big part of the waste ground and the old bulldozers and pile drivers were bashing away.

They were putting a tower block up, or a supermarket – anybody's guess. One half of the town was getting demolished and the other half was being turned into a shopping centre.

All of a sudden, I met Steve. He was by himself, watching the big crane. It was fantastic to see that massive iron arm come round all worked by a bloke in a glass box so far up he looked like a bit of Lego.

'Hallo, Mike,' he said.

'Hallo, Steve.'

We went into the fast food place and had a milk shake. Steve was paying. He flashed a five. He must have seen my eyes.

'Earned that.'

'Get off.'

'Did 'n' all. Went out with our kid and Uncle Bill.'

'Hey, what doing?'

'Scrapping. He's got this old truck. They go round places picking up metal. You know, like when they close a mill down. Uncle Bill hears – on the wire, like. He goes round, whips it all out before you can blink.'

Steve started laughing.

'Last month he was too quick. He had this load of gear on the truck when the owner turned up. The place wasn't closed down yet. Uncle Bill asked him for £50 to put it all back. But he fetched the Law.'

I started laughing. Then I stopped when Steve said:

'He lets me come sometimes, and help. Pays me. Want to come next week?'

Before I had time to think what they'd say at home, I answered.

'Right on.'

'See you, then, Mike.'

'See you, Steve.'

3

On My Own

Next Saturday, I had to be a bit crafty. I had to be up early enough to get clear of Andy and up round to Steve's place where the scrappie waggon was going to be waiting. But not too early for our Sis to notice and start saying things like:

'And where's he off to this time in the morning?'

And starting Mum off, asking:

'Yes, Mike, where are you going? Aren't you going to wait for Andy?'

So I was planning to slide up about quarter past eight, pour downstairs, slip through the kitchen, scooping up a bowl of Supernosh on my way, and then out through the back yard, muttering as I went:

'Got to rush. Tell Andy I'll see him later.'

It was brilliant. But then I am ace at working things out in advance.

The only trouble was, I overslept, didn't I? The

first thing I knew was Mum shouting up the stairs.

'You Mike, are you going to stop there all day?'

I staggered up, rubbing my eyes. Then I remembered. I was going to be early. I was going to get clear of Andy and meet Steve and go off on the scrappie wagon. I grabbed for my jeans, stepped into them, and missed, picked myself up and tried again. Then I decided to get my pyjamas off first.

At last I succeeded. I got the show on the road. But I was too late for Steve. The road in front of the flats was empty. The truck had gone. Of course it had. They couldn't hang about when they had to pull the town to bits before sunset, could they?

Fed up, I trundled off again down the road. I was half way home when I realised that I hadn't seen Andy, crash helmet, stunt bike and all. He was nowhere. I found myself wandering past the shelters. There wasn't much waste ground left now. Another big fence in that yellow coloured, splintery wood had been rushed up right across the bike track. What a life!

There was a crowd of kids, all juniors, hanging about, some with bikes, some waiting hopefully. But no Andy. Where was he? And what was I wondering for? I didn't want to see him, did I?

The trouble was, there was nobody else. No one, nowhere. I turned round again and headed – where? Not home. I wouldn't be welcome there, with all the housework going on. On the other

hand, I might be too welcome. I'll say one thing for our Mum. She's very modern in her outlook. She doesn't mind blokes helping out in the house.

I wandered off towards the park. The clock over the Co-op said ten o'clock. Was that all? What was I going to do with myself till dinner time? No Steve, no Sandra. Ranji gone. Not even flipping Andy. What a life.

Why I went that way, I can't think. It's up hill all the way, and it was getting warmer. Which made me more fed up as I climbed the slope. Mountaineering was never my favourite sport. By the foot of the big grass slope, I stopped and sat on the ground. The twisted branches of the old oak tree, covered in leaves, stretched out over me. The twigs always start putting out extra shoots when you're well into summer. It was only a few weeks to the holidays. Fat lot of good that was, I thought.

The branches moved and rustled. Which was funny. There was no wind. Then something hit me, hard, right on the end of my nose – an oak apple or such. A second later it happened again. And somebody laughed.

I jumped up. Cheek! Messing about in our oak tree was bad enough. But this was. . . .

Then I saw, staring at me through the branches, a familiar brown face, with a wide grin. I let out a shout:

'Ranji!'

17

4

Sandra's Secret

I gave a great yell, charged up the slope and swung out on to the main branch of the oak. Ranji was sitting in his usual place at the end of the bough. And there in the middle, swinging her legs and grinning like a Cheshire cat, was Sandra. She burst out laughing when she saw my face.

'Surprise! Surprise! We came round to your place earlier on. Your Sis said you'd sneaked off and wouldn't tell anyone where you were going.'

'Oh – er,' I started. Then I changed my mind about telling them I'd been planning to go out with the scrappies. I changed the subject.

'Where did *you* spring from?' I asked Ranji.

He shrugged. 'That new job Dad got – it folded. So we came back here. We're all living with my Uncle, and Dad's working in his shop, helping out.'

He stopped and looked at us.

'Well, it's better than nowt,' said Sandra.

I nodded. It was.

'Hey, are you coming back to our school, Ranji?'

'I don't know. We have to go in and see them. I may not start until after the holidays, any road.'

'That's great,' I said. 'The gang's together again. Except Andy. Where's he?'

Sandra made a face.

'He's with our Dad. He's got him for this week.'

'Hey, how d'you mean?'

'My dear little brother has been getting himself into trouble. Been on his own too much. Dad's away all the time. So either Andy looks after himself, or I get lumbered.'

'Join the club,' I said. 'He's been hanging round our place.'

Sandra nodded. 'That's weekends. But listen, every day, I have to come home right across town to be there when our Andy comes home for his tea.'

'Hey,' said Ranji. 'Why don't you switch to our school? Your kid'll be moving up there next year.'

Sandra laughed. 'You tell our Dad that. He thinks your school's the pits. He reckons St Winifred's is a class school – if only he knew!'

'There's nowt wrong with our school,' I said. 'Well, not much. You tell him, Sandra, he wants you to look after your kid, he lets you switch schools.'

'Dead easy, eh, Mike?' Sandra punched me on the arm.

Then she went on: 'Hey, listen. We didn't come up here to rabbit on about our kid.'

'No,' put in Ranji. 'Mike, Sandra's found this fantastic place, right across the moors by Penfold Forest.'

'Don't know why they call it a Forest anyway,' I said. 'There's only a couple of dozen trees there.'

'Anyway, there's this little valley, with . . .' began Ranji. Suddenly, I noticed Sandra's face. She looked ready to clobber somebody.

'Do you two mind? This was *my* story.'

She glared at us both.

'Ah, diddums, Sandra,' I said.

'Right,' she answered. 'That's better. I was out there with the Harriers, last weekend. We ran right over to Penfold. And, while we were running, I saw this place in the distance. Anyway, on the way back, I made a detour and went closer. There's an old pond, all dried up, at the top, and a sluice, you know, like gates where they let the water through, then a long wooden slide thing, running right down on pillars. And down below in this little valley, there's some old houses, by the side of a stream. All empty and mysterious.'

She paused a bit and looked at us.

'I reckoned – how about us going over there, next weekend?'

She looked apologetic.

'You see. I've got to have our Andy with me, so I can't go out running . . .'

'So you thought you'd get us mugs along, eh, Sandra?' I said. 'Seven miles across the moors. You must be joking.'

She looked at me in a funny way, almost upset.

'Sorry. Anyway, we don't have to walk seven miles. You can get the Penfold bus and drop off at the top by the Forest, it's only a mile or so . .'

'Huh.' I interrupted. 'How much is *so*?'

Ranji stood up, balancing on the bough. He made it rock up and down.

'Anyway, I think the gang ought to do this to help Sandra. And who knows, it could turn out to be really exciting.'

That turned out to be the understatement of the year.

5

Ranji *v* Steve

Sandra, Ranji and I climbed down from the tree and strolled back through the park. Today was turning out fine after all. The gang was together again – even if we did have to share Sandra with the bandy-legged men in running shorts. And we had our own secret place to go to when the holidays started.

I felt so good, I decided to push my luck. Just as we reached the park gate, I said, casually,

'How about it if my mate Steve joins in?'

Ranji shook his head.

'Not much, Mike. Steve may be OK to you, but his brother's a big ape. I don't trust them.'

I turned to Sandra. She hesitated.

'I don't know, Mike. You know that family get up to dodgy things. My Dad says their Uncle Bill's been in lumber before – you know, nicking things and selling them back. They reckon he'll take anything that isn't bolted down.'

'Ah, come on,' I said. 'What has that got to do with Steve coming with us – you know, joining the gang, like?'

Ranji shook his head again. This time he was frowning.

'No way, Mike, no way. Hey,' he said, suddenly, 'I have to shoot. I'm late already.'

He turned up the hill and ran, waving as he went. Sandra looked at me.

'Sorry, Mike. I think you'll have to leave it for now.'

I shrugged. 'I don't really see what Ranji's got against Steve.'

She stared at me.

'Well, Mike. Look at it this way. Would they let Ranji join their mob?'

'OK, Sandra. I get it. Still . . . .'

Sandra took hold of the sleeve of my jacket.

'Look Mike, leave it for now. Till the holidays come. Maybe things'll sort themselves out.'

'OK,' I said.

But they didn't. They got more complicated.

6

Ranji *v* Steve, Round 2

The last week of term was coming up. Everybody was getting more and more wound up, dashing here and there, just waiting for the end, wondering why we had to come in to school at all, when there weren't even proper lessons any more.

This particular day, just after lunch, Steve and I were rushing down the corridor off the main hall. As a matter of fact, he'd just nicked half a bar of chocolate and I was chasing him. We dashed round this corner and nearly ran over Ranji.

'Hey Ranj – what . . . .?'

He shook his head, quickly. Then I saw who else was there. It was like a meeting outside this door. Old Tweedy Harris, tall and grey with that screwed up, sarky look of his. He's head of Second Year, worse luck. And then there was this Indian family, a little lady with two small girls, shy and giggling. And on the other side of Tweedy, who had his back to us, was this bloke, long and thin. His wrists stood out of the sleeves of his jacket when he spoke, his arms waving. And he was mad about something. I knew it must be Ranji's Dad.

We were just sneaking past when I heard Tweedy's voice, all quiet and smarmy.

'I think there must be some misunderstanding . . . er, just one of those linguistic problems.'

If Ranji's Dad could have strangled Tweedy there and then I'm sure he would have. Instead he raised his voice. He stammered a bit.

'There – is only – one linguistic problem, sir. You are not understanding what I am saying . . . .'

It was the sound of his voice, so angry, and the sight of Tweedy's face, that sneering look when he puts somebody down. I suppose Steve couldn't help it. He started sniggering.

Tweedy Harris looked round. Now he had a chance to really show he was boss around here.

'You, boy. What are you gawping at? Wipe that grin off your face and clear out.'

He pointed. Steve and I ran, Steve still with his hand over his mouth.

But, as we ran, I caught sight of Ranji, glaring at Steve. And if looks could kill. . . .

7

A Weird Place on the Moors

That Saturday morning we all piled into the bus and headed for Penfold. First of all, of course, I had to go through the routine with Mum: 'Where are you going? What are you up to?'

I said something vague about exploring some old places up at Penfold Forest. She looked a bit doubtful at first, but when I said I was going with Sandra, Ranji and Andy, she was making up the lunch pack before you could wink.

If only she knew. If only *we* knew.

It was a great day. There was mist in the early morning, but I didn't see much of that, did I, with my head down. But the sun came through later, and the sky cleared. It was due to be another scorcher. The old people on the bus were going on about their cauliflowers and so on, there was going to be a drought, an' all. But for us, it was just holiday weather.

The moors were greeny brown with the rocks and fern, changing to purple in the distance, where the hills were higher. There were sparrowhawks hovering over the ground and in the distance, through the bus windows, you could hear that funny noise the snipe makes, like a lawn mower.

Sandra and I chatted away. She was telling me more about this strange place she'd found over by Penfold. There used to be a forest there at one time. It stretched for miles, she reckoned. But people had cut the trees down for fires and then the sheep had grazed it all flat like a bowling green. So now there were just a few trees left and these mysterious buildings, like a deserted village.

'A ghost town, eh, Andy?' I said. But he didn't answer. He was having a grump.

Sandra grinned. 'He wanted to go up the shelters with his bike. But he had to go with his rotten old sister.'

'Anyway, Andy,' I nudged him. 'They're fencing the shelters off now. You couldn't go there, see.'

'Big deal,' he muttered. 'I'd have found somewhere else. I didn't want to traipse all over the flaming moors looking at a lot of old rubbish. But Dad says I've got to go with her.'

He jerked his thumb at Sandra. I thought she'd laugh. But instead she snapped, her eyes flashing.

'If you think I *want* to take you out, our Andrew, you have got another think coming. I've been lumbered with you. So you can belt up!'

27

That shut him up. She wasn't funny when she was really angry.

So I thought I'd carry on the good work and talk to Ranji, who hadn't said a word either, since we set out.

'Hey, Ranji. Your Dad was mad at Harris. What was it all about?'

He looked out of the window. I could see it still hurt.

'Nothing, Mike. Forget it. It's sorted out now.'

'Hey, Ranji. Steve and I couldn't help seeing it, and it did seem a bit funny.'

He turned sharply to me.

'You think so? You wouldn't have, if it had been your Dad.'

'Hey, I'm sorry, Ranji.'

Ranji stuck out his under lip.

'I wouldn't have minded all that much if *you* had laughed. It was Taylor. That's different.'

That shut me up. We all kept quiet while the bus drove on over the moors.

8

Andy's Crazy Slide

Just then, the bus pulled up, and we all tumbled out. Nobody talked at first. Sandra led the way off the road and up a track through some trees. It was getting hot now and when we got out on the open moor, and started to climb up towards a ridge, there was no shelter from the sun. After about a mile, we were all sweating and Andy wanted to stop and get out his can of coke.

'Well, you're not,' said his sister. 'It's not much farther. You can wait till we get there.'

'Not far, huh.' He glared at her. 'I know your "not far". Another flaming five miles.'

Ranji put his arm round Andy's shoulders.

'Cheer up. You carry me up the hill and I'll carry you down.'

Andy shoved Ranji away, then burst out laughing. You couldn't really be angry with Ranji when he was joking.

I was relieved. Ranji seemed to be in a good mood again. He started to sing:

'Climb every mountain,
Ford every stream
Trifle for breakfast,
Pork chops and cream.'

We all fell about. Andy got so excited, he charged ahead to the crest of the rise. Then he came running back, yelling.

'Come on, come on. It's fantastic.'

We struggled up behind him to the top. Below us, the ground dropped away and the path twisted through a great mass of bracken. From over on the right, came a stream that curved round to spread out into a kind of marsh with mud and patches of water, clumps of grass and reeds.

It was like a dried up pond or pool, and over on the far side were two brick pillars and a broken, rusty iron gate, like a portcullis on a castle.

'Hey, that's the sluice for letting the water out,' I shouted.

'Ah, well, somebody left it open, didn't they?' said Ranji.

'Where's all the water gone to, though?' asked Andy, as we hurried down to the side of the stream and skirted the marshy pond bed.

'You wait and see,' called his sister, who was in the lead. I could see that she was really excited herself, even when she was doing the big sister bit.

'Here, look!' yelled Andy as he reached the sluice and climbed on the nearest pillar, pointing down in front of him.

We hurried on. Below us was yet another valley, with steeper sides. The stream bed curved down in a wide sweep. But now, what with the drought and the pool at the top silting up, there was only a trickle of water pushing through the gap in the broken sluice gates and running gently down the slope.

On either side of the valley were ruined buildings, like farm houses. Right at the foot of the hill two of them stood at right angles, bigger than the others, almost as big as a factory. One had the roof broken in, with great holes in the slates and rotting beams showing through. But the other looked intact. There were even glass panes in some of the windows.

'Look at that, now,' Andy was squealing.

We stared. Stretching out from the other side of the sluice gates was a brick and stone channel, now choked with muck and grass. This led into another channel, like a helter-skelter slide, made of wood, standing on brick columns, curving down the hill alongside and above the stream, then vanishing round the end of the biggest works building.

'What is it?' demanded Andy.

'Looks like those chutes they have at the pits for sending coal down,' I answered. 'Like when they sort it.'

'Get off,' said Sandra. 'It's water that goes down there, if anything.'

'Well, what do they want to send water down there for?'

'Easy, isn't it. When they wanted their bath on Saturday night, they closed the sluice, then when the water ran into the chute out of the pond, they ran down hill, taking their clothes off as they went, and stood at the bottom and let it fall down all over them, like a shower. . . .'

Suddenly, Sandra stopped.

'You, Andy. What are you up to?'

We all turned, but it was too late. Before we could stop him, Andy had climbed off the sluice posts, run along the brick channel, sat down on the chute and pushed himself off.

He gave a great shout as he tobogganed down. But it died out as he reached the first bend. There was a splintering crash and, with a terrific howl, Andy just vanished.

9

Sandra's Discovery

We jumped down off the sluice gate wall like a shot and rushed down the grass slope under the chute, falling all over each other. Sandra was as white as a sheet. That idiot Andy might have killed himself.

But, he hadn't. There he was, below the third brick pillar, half way down the hill. He'd come right through the wooden planks of the chute and was hanging on by his fingers from the edge of the hole he'd made, kicking and screaming at the top of his voice.

The moment we saw he wasn't really hurt, we fell about. Ranji and I punched each other and rolled round on the grass. Till Sandra, who was red in the face with anger now, shouted at us to help him down. He was only three feet from the ground but he was too scared to let go. It took all three of us to lift him off. What a lump. And as he came down we all collapsed with him on top and his foot

33

hit my nose. It was agony. I could have clobbered him.

I didn't need to. Sandra helped him up with one hand and then clouted him over the earhole with the other. He howled.

'Hey, San, what was that for?' asked Ranji, catching hold of Andy as he went for his sister like a tank, both fists going.

'He drives me up the wall,' she yelled. I could see tears in her eyes.

'Are you OK, Andy?' I asked, just to change the subject.

He felt all round himself and nodded. 'I think I've got splinters in me bum,' he said.

We all began to laugh, and Sandra took charge again.

'Right, let's get down there and inspect this place,' she said. We jumped and slithered down the rest of the hill and came out in a big yard, covered with grass and weeds and littered with great lumps of timber.

'Look at them, like railway sleepers.'

'No, bigger, more like ships' timbers. Must be a foot across.'

There wasn't much to inspect in the first building. The roof had dropped in. Rafters stuck up in the air, mouldy plaster and wallpaper hung down in strips, and here and there big black stains spread up the brickwork.

'People lived here,' said Ranji. 'Those are

fireplaces.'

'Were. Couldn't have had much room, could they?'

'Oh, they lived three families to a room then.'

'Some people still do.'

We scrabbled around in the rubbish on the ground, but there wasn't much. An old brush handle, a saucepan with a hole in it. Then Ranji held up something, like a bowl with a handle.

'Hey, what's that?' asked Andy.

Sandra hooted.

'That's a chamber pot.'

'What's that for?'

'Oh they used 'em at night to save going out. They had the loo at the bottom of the garden.'

'You're kidding.'

'Not.'

'Come on,' I said, 'put the World Cup down and let's look in that big place.'

The other building stood at right angles to the ruined cottages and it seemed all in one piece, though some of the glass in the windows was smashed. Leading off the yard were two huge doors, thick and heavy, with patches of faded green paint on the rotting planks.

'Ah, it's locked,' moaned Andy pulling at the rusty padlock and chain that hung across the timbers. Then he grinned and suddenly swung on it. With a tear and a crunch he was on his back, two chain lengths in his hands.

I could see Sandra grit her teeth. But she said nothing. Andy's crazy swing had pulled one door away from the other. Grinding and creaking, it swung back and flapped against the outer wall. From inside came a rush of rotten, dank air. Beyond we could see strange shapes, looming up, one after another, in the gloom.

Half afraid, we stopped between the daylight and the dark.

'Hey, what is it?' breathed Andy.

Ranji eased past me and bent down. He was struggling with something behind the door. There was a grating noise, then he heaved the other half-door back. More light came in and now we could see what looked like a big hall, with no ceiling – just rafters. Stretching away to the end which was almost pitch dark, were a row of rusting machines with dozens of wires and cylinders in lines.

'I know what these are,' said Ranji. 'They're looms. It's a mill. Look.' He pointed upwards. 'That long iron thing, that's the shaft, they got their power from that.'

'Power?' I demanded. 'Where's the motor, then?'

'Look over there,' shouted Andy, dashing away to the end of the big hall, stumbling and jumping over fallen lumps of brick and wood. We followed. Beyond the machines was an open space, then we jerked to a stop in front of a great hole in the floor.

'Hey, it's like those inspection pits they have in garages – and look at all that stuff.'

Massive iron cog wheels and shafts were piled up against one another.

'Look at the teeth on those wheels. Must be six inches, like a ship's engines.'

'No, it's like a giant's clock works,' said Andy. We laughed. He was right.

'They're gears,' Ranji pointed. 'Those teeth lock into one another. One wheel turns the next, and they make the belts go that run the looms.'

'Ah, but where's the engine? They couldn't have electricity down here. It's miles from anywhere. There's no cable. And there's no mill chimney, neither.'

Sandra had climbed into the pit and was balancing on an iron shaft like a giant pipe. She pointed to where it ran into the wall through a narrow, black arch in the bricks.

Crouching down until she was almost lying on the shaft, head twisted inside the dark gap, she stared for what seemed to be minutes. Then she drew back her head.

'That's fantastic,' she gasped. 'I've never seen anything like that.'

10

The Great Wheel

She clambered out of the pit and we gathered round her. Her face and hair were smeared with oil and grime.

'It's like a big tower on the other side. High walls. And right in the middle, there's this massive big wheel. Big iron spokes, this thick, and high. Must be thirty foot high. It's like one of those wheels at the fair ground. Only it's got steps on it like a staircase.'

'Let's have a look,' demanded Andy, starting to climb down. Sandra grabbed him.

'No, not you, mate. This time you'll be breaking your neck.'

If looks could kill! There'd have been a fight on the spot, when I had an inspiration.

'Hey, there's forced to be a way in on the other side. I mean nobody could crawl through that shaft hole, could they?'

'Good thinking, Mike.'

We all turned at once and pushed past one another, out of the big double doorway, into the yard and round the corner. Sure enough, at the end of the old mill was like a high brick tower, stuck right up close against the main building. We jerked to a halt.

'That's where the chute runs down to,' yelled Andy, pointing up. Sure enough, the timber channel coming down the hillside from the old sluice pool ended on the flat top of the tower.

'Hey, what d'you reckon?' he said, grabbing Ranji's arm. 'If I'd have gone all the way down the chute, I'd have ended up on top of that wheel inside there. Hey, like Charlie Chaplin in that film, going round and round.'

'Not much you wouldn't,' I said. 'You'd have smashed the whole thing to splinters.'

Ranji was round at the other side of the tower already.

Round the corner we found ourselves in an open space with grass and bushes. Beyond them I could hear the sound of the stream gurgling along down in its bed. It wasn't very loud. There couldn't be much water there after the hot summer.

Ranji was right. The big tower did have a door in it, like a church door with an arch and not very high.

'Come on, let's get it open, then.'

Ranji shook his head. 'It's blocked. Part of this

wall's come down and it's blocking it. There must be three thicknesses of brick. It's massive.'

Sandra studied the heap of bricks and mortar lying across the door.

'We could shift that,' she said. 'Won't take us more than an hour if we all go at it.'

Without thinking we all threw ourselves at the pile. It wasn't a good idea. The chunks of brickwork were jagged and heavy. We dropped lumps on our toes, cut our hands, banged into each other. And, guess what? Andy very soon decided he'd had enough.

'We're never going to clear all this. Anyway, I'm hungry.'

'Trust you to start objecting when it comes to a bit of work,' snapped his sister. 'Just like at home.'

'Oh shut your ——,' replied her brother, full of charm.

Ranji and I looked at one another.

'Let's eat our lunch,' we both said at once.

We moved over to the bank of the stream, wiped our hands on the grass, admired our cuts and bruises and then opened our sandwiches. We sat there, back to back in the warm sun, eating and drinking. This was the part I liked best.

Ranji looked up the slope to the head of the valley.

'See how it works,' he said.

'How?' said Andy with his mouth full.

'Well, when that sluice gate's closed up there, the water fills the pond. Then they open the gate to the chute channel.'

'There wasn't a gate. It was open.'

I could see now why Sandra found her little brother a pain.

Ranji raised his eyebrows and went on. 'When there *was* a gate, they opened it and let the water into the chute. It shoots down the channel, going faster and faster. Then it runs through on to the wheel inside that tower.'

'Hey,' said Sandra. 'That's what those steps are for. You know . . .'

'That's it – paddles, they call them,' I put in.

Ranji looked at us both with a pained

expression.

'The water turns the wheel. The big iron shaft goes through the wall and turns the gear wheels and – bingo – all the looms start going.'

'Except they don't,' I said. 'They're all in bits.'

'That wheel isn't,' said Sandra. 'It looked all in one piece . . .' Suddenly she turned to me, her eyes lighting up.

'Hey, d'you reckon we could get it working?'

Ranji and I grinned.

'We'll have to shift all those bricks first.'

'Yeah, and clear some of that old iron in that pit.'

'Yeah, and mend that part of the chute your brother put his big fat bum through.'

She jumped up: 'We've got all the holidays, now!'

'What about your hairy-legged mates in the Harriers?'

'They won't miss me for a week or two.'

We started to laugh. Then came Andy's grumpy voice.

'Well, you won't catch me humping flipping stones all –'

'Shut up!' we all yelled at once.

11

I Find Out A Thing or Two

The last week of term dragged. I wouldn't be seeing the others till Saturday, when we planned to make our first big expedition out to the secret mill. That's what we called it. It looked secret. It didn't seem as though anyone had bothered with it for donkey's years. So we reckoned it was ours.

Sandra promised she'd get some tools from home. Her Dad wasn't too bothered as long as she kept Andy out of trouble. He never expected *her* to get into trouble.

I was going to get extra grub from home. I didn't exactly tell Mum what we were up to. There was this place over the moors, I said. She thought that meant hiking and hiking was healthy, wasn't it? Well, anyway.

So it was all arranged. All I could do was hang about waiting for Saturday. I had to sort of avoid Steve. We hadn't spoken much since I'd missed going out with the scrappies. I'd have liked to invite him to come with us. But I had a feeling he'd say no. And I knew Ranji wasn't having it. So I was stuck.

But I did have one brilliant idea. I get one a week or so. Friday afternoon I nipped down to the library. Not the ordinary library, the reference part where they do joined up reading. Our Sis worked there. And I had to box clever.

'Sis,' I said across the counter where she sat with her posh new computer screen and keyboard. For all I knew she could be playing Space Invaders. 'We're going hiking up Penfold Forest.'

'Pull the other one,' she said, cheerfully. Now I could see why Andy got annoyed with Sandra. I ignored her wit and went on. 'Have you got like, a guide book?'

She burst out laughing, then put her hand over her mouth. There was a big notice over her head which said, QUIET PLEASE. PEOPLE MAY BE STUDYING.

'Stop messing about, our Sis,' I said, 'I'm serious.'

She grinned: 'No kid. Look.' She got up and walked across to one of the shelves and then came back with a tatty little grey book. 'There's this. It's called Penfold Peregrinations.'

'You're putting me on.'

She drew her hand across her throat.

'It was written years and years ago, by this old bloke. It's got half a dozen walks with maps and

45

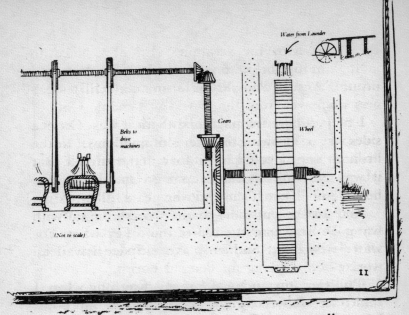

Water from Launder

Belts to
drive
machines

Gears

Wheel

(Not to scale)

II

bits and pieces of information. Do you really want to look at it, our kid?'

I nodded. She left the desk and came back a minute later with the book.

'Look after it now. Use one of the desks over there. You can't take it out. It's the only copy we have.'

I started to look through the book. It was funny, all right. All kinds of peculiar phrases, long words and those weird sketches that the old bloke had done of ancient trees, old stone columns, out of the way houses and bridges. There was even one of a gibbet on top of a hill where they used to hang people. It was a great life in the old days. I was just about to give it back to our Sis, when I saw, at the foot of a page:

'. . . . . just below the remnants of the erstwhile proud Forest of Penfold is Hargreaves' Mill, which gets its power from the waters of Pendale Ghill.'

I flipped over the page and there it was. On one side was a drawing of the old buildings. Not a brilliant one. I could have done better myself. But it was our mill all right. And on the other page he'd done a sketch showing the gears, all working.

And on the outside was the wooden chute with water pouring into the top of the tower where the water wheel sat. Suddenly I could see how it all worked.

I jumped up and was on my way out when I remembered Sis said I couldn't borrow the book. Then I had another brilliant idea. I nipped up to the desk, borrowed paper and pen off Sis and copied out some of the sketches and notes. She stared when I handed the book back. She was dying to ask what I was up to, but I didn't let on.

On my way out, going through the part where they have the stands with video cassettes, I was holding the paper, looking at the sketches of our mill, when I nearly ran into someone.

'Hey Mike, what've you got there?'

It was Steve.

12

Trouble with Steve

I quickly slipped the paper into my pocket.

'Let's have a look.'

'Oh, it's nothing, Steve. Just something I copied for a project at school.' I jerked my thumb over my shoulder at the reference library.

'You creep, working on a project last day of term. Don't believe you. You're ligging.'

'Not,' I said, looking away.

We were outside the library now and walking along the pavement. Steve nudged me.

'What're you doing in the break, Mike?'

I shrugged. I was really embarrassed now.

'Oh, don't know. Messing about.'

I changed tack.

'What are you doing, Steve?'

He shrugged.

'Not much. Uncle Bill's away. Got something big going somewhere. Even our Sam hasn't got a look in. But I expect he'll be out with the scrappie waggon, sometime. Want to come with?'

'Might.'

He stared at me.

'Hey, you've got something going. Why aren't you telling me?'

I didn't know which way to look. We were walking along now, near the shelters.

'Look at that,' I pointed. 'All fenced off. We'll soon have *nowhere* decent to go.'

'Please yourself,' said Steve. I could see from the frown on his face he was getting narked with me. 'You don't want me with, do you?'

I stopped and took a deep breath. But he got in first.

'It's your Paki mate, isn't it?' he said.

'His family's from India, and anyway, he was born here,' I said. I didn't know why I was arguing.

'Same difference. He's saying no, so I don't get to come with.'

I made myself look at Steve.

'Look, that day at school, when Tweedy Harris was being snotty with Ranji's Dad.'

'Oh, that. Well it was a bit of a giggle.' He imitated the accent: 'You are not understanding me.'

'Well, it wasn't a giggle for Ranji.' I was getting annoyed with Steve now.

'Big deal.'

'Well, it wasn't, Steve. I mean. . .' I thought a bit. 'When they make you feel small at school, you're small. But when they make your parents feel small – you vanish.'

'Ah, lot of fuss about nowt,' said Steve.

'Come on Steve, look,' I urged him. 'Why can't you tell Ranji you didn't really mean to laugh at his Dad? You wouldn't like it if he laughed at your Dad.'

Steve snapped: 'Nobody, but nobody laughs at my Dad.'

'Big deal. Come on Steve. Just have a word with Ranji . . .'

He stared at me.

'Get lost, mate, get lost.'

13

Even if it Kills Us?

Early next day we were all sitting in the old oak. I had my bit of paper from the library. I was bragging about it and, to be fair, they were impressed. Though Sandra couldn't resist a few sarky remarks about my technical drawings. I ignored her and went on.

'There's always been a water mill there. First it was a corn mill – then it was a log mill,' I explained.

'That's when they cut Penfold Forest down,' interrupted Sandra.

'Who's telling this? Then in 1849, this bloke Hargreaves had a big woollen mill in Penfold.'

'Hey,' squealed Andy. 'I can see why they call them mills, now.'

'Wake up at the back there,' I said.

Sandra punched me: 'Admit it, Mike, you never knew before that mills for cotton and mills for flour really came from the same thing.'

I took a deep breath.

'Am I going to be allowed to continue. . . ?'

'Yeah,' said Ranji, 'stop interrupting yourself and get on.'

I did.

'Anyway. There was this big strike. They brought the Army in.'

'Nowt new in that . . .'

'They brought the Army in. So somebody burnt the mill down. So Hargreaves' son moved out to this place in the Forest, in 1870, and started up a small mill with six looms.'

'That's it. There are six looms there now,' said Ranji.

'So how come it's all falling to bits?' demanded Andy.

'I'm coming to that. It says here: "Water from the mill pound . . ." '

'What's that?'

'That's the pond up the hill. "Water flows down the launder . . ." '

'Get off, you mean chute.'

I waved my piece of paper.

'It says here it's called a launder.'

'Hey, maybe a small one's called a launderette.'

I gave them all a withering glance.

' "The water entering the top of the wheelhouse, strikes the paddles of the overshot wheel. The power is transmitted via the gears. . . . ." '

'Oh, give over, Mike – get to the point. Why did it close down?'

'In 1924, they had a terrific freak rain storm. The wheelhouse outlet was blocked and the mill flooded. It was annual holiday week. Most people were away . . . pretty well everything, gear and cloth was ruined.'

'So that stuff's been there for over 60 years,' said Sandra. 'Hey, if we could get it going, they'd give us a Queen's Medal, or something like . . .'

'Big deal,' I said.

'Never mind about that,' put in Ranji. 'I just want to see that wheel go round.'

'Yeah,' said Andy, 'and ride on the paddles.'

'You never,' his sister grinned at him. 'There isn't room. We'd be scraping you off the walls.'

'Charming.'

'Anyway,' I took charge. 'Thing is, what do we do first?'

'Fix up that chute thing,' shouted Andy.

His sister shook her head.

'Waste of time. You have to have water in the pool. So we have to mend the sluice gate first or all the water'll go on running out.'

'If that gear pit is all jammed up, how's the wheel going to turn?' I demanded. 'So we have to start there.'

Ranji shook his head.

'Uh uh. First thing we have to do is finish clearing those bricks and get into the wheelhouse.'

We all looked at each other. Andy's mouth turned down at the corners.

'Ah, we'll never get it all done.'

'Get off with you,' said Sandra. 'We've got all summer, haven't we? We'll have that wheel going round before we go back to school, even if it kills us.'

We all laughed. But later on, I remembered those last words.

14

Locked Out

So, we started the big job of getting our secret mill going again. We didn't call it Hargreaves' Mill. After all, they'd let it go to rack and ruin. We'd found it, and finders keepers. No one else seemed to care about it – out on the moors there, all battered and neglected.

Almost every day we could we'd set off to Penfold. We'd have sandwiches with. At first, Mum made them up for me. Then she left me to get on with them myself while she got off to work.

Sometimes we'd get the bus. But when we were short of money we went on our bikes. Once or twice we got a lift from a truck. It was great. Every day would start misty. Sometimes we would be shivering when we waited on the road. But as we travelled the sun would break through and as we climbed up to the ridge it would be warm on our backs.

There would be the valley below, the marshy mill pool, the broken-down sluice gate. We'd break into a run and charge like an army waving our gear, shovels and hammers, until we came up short by the sluice wall and looked down the launder channel. There beneath us would be the stream bed, the wheelhouse, the old broken buildings. Our stronghold.

The easy bits got done first. We found some wood strips and repaired the launder channel where Andy put his bum through. Some wood strips nailed over the gap made it just about watertight. Then we tackled the pile of stones and brick blocking the wheelhouse door. But that was heavy work, and we all got cuts and bruises. When a lump of brickwork turns over on your ankle it's agony. So we took turns, two of us shifting bricks, two of us taking timber up the hill. Ranji worked out that if we could fix several planks down the slots in the wall where the old sluice gate had been, this would form a kind of dam so the water would build up in the pond.

It was slow going. And of course Andy got fed up first. Once or twice he sneaked off with his bike to the Rec and didn't turn up.

Sandra would go spare and chase after him. She always knew where to find him when he sloped off. He'd be showing off on his bike with that crowd of kids from the juniors. He was top dog this year and he knew it. But he wasn't top dog for his sister. He was her kid brother.

'I'll wrap that bike round his neck.'

'Can't we just leave him?' I said one day.

'No way, Dad won't let me. I'm lumbered.'

'It's not fair.'

Ranji looked pompous. 'The oldest child has to look after the younger ones.'

'All right for you, mate. You've got two cuddly little sisters and a Mam and Dad as well.'

'Come on then,' I said. 'Andy comes with us whether he likes it or not.'

And he came with us. But often he'd get fed up and wander off up the hill and play in the mud round the marshy mill pond. One day, when we were taking a break for a drink of coke, he came yelling down the hill. He tripped up and rolled down knocking himself silly on a stone. Then he picked himself up.

'It's filling up.'

'What is?' snapped his sister, pushing her hair away from her eyes.

'The pool, stupid.'

'Get off. How do you know?'

' 'Cause I put a stick at the edge to mark it, and it's come up three inches.'

'Big deal.' We all looked at one another.

Sandra glared at her brother.

'Come on you, help me carry some more of these bricks.'

But, the next day, when we came over the ridge,

we all stopped and stared. Light flashed on something up ahead and we saw the water *had* crept up. Some of the grass clumps were almost covered by a white sheet that reflected the sun.

We gave a great cheer and galloped down the hill. Sure enough, Andy's stick marker was nearly covered.

That day we worked like demons pulling and shoving at the bricks blocking the wheelhouse door. We saved time by not humping them away, but piled them up to one side in a square stack. At first we did it neatly, then as we got more excited we just slung them on top as fast as we could. And slowly we were getting there.

We all piled in, pulling and shoving, grunting and heaving, passing the lumps from one to another, till at last the space in front of the door was clear. Then Sandra jumped forward and grabbed the big handle on the door and gave a great pull.

'Open Sesame,' she yelled.

The iron ring snapped off in her hands and she flew back, knocking Ranji over. But the door had opened an inch or two, and I took her place tugging at the edge. A great jerk and a sudden pain as I broke two of my nails. I turned in despair to the others.

'It won't budge.'

Behind us, Andy grouched.

'Flipping heck. Might have known. Let's go home.'

15

The Mill Pool Fills Up

The sound of Andy's voice set his sister off. She grabbed up the spade we'd brought with us, leapt at the door and shoved the blade into the narrow gap. Then she pulled violently back and forward and as she pulled she swore. I never knew they used words like that at St Winifred's.

'Come on!' she shouted.

We joined in, getting a hand hold on the spade handle. As we did the door creaked and whined on its hinges as if it was in pain.

'It's giving.'

Andy shoved round the side with a lump of timber which he thrust into the gap. Just in time, because the spade blade was buckling. Now we all pulled on this new lever. The door was opening, a bit wider, three inches, six inches. Then, at a foot, it would not budge any further. It took all our strength to stop it snapping back into place.

'Quick!' gasped Ranji. He dodged back and came up with another lump of timber. He forced it in between door and wall at head height. There was a crunch as we let go. The wedge buckled but held. The door was open – just enough room to squeeze inside.

Ranji turned to Sandra and bowed.

'After you, madame.'

One by one we struggled in through the gap. We stared. It was incredible. We were inside a big chamber with brick walls that rose up like cliffs into half darkness at the top, where sunlight came through in narrow beams through an iron grill.

They shone on the wheel, like a big spidery monster with iron legs that stretched out from under our feet in all directions upwards and downwards. We were standing on a three foot ledge with a rail. The wheel rose up to the roof above and plunged down into the pit below.

'It's massive. Must be thirty foot up and down.'

'Easy. Hey, think about it going round.'

'Yeah, look at those wooden steps. They must be five feet across.'

'They're paddles, like one of those river steamers.'

I pointed up to where the sun shone down.

'That's where the water comes through, down that narrow gap at the end of the grid. Then it hits the paddles, turns the wheel and runs away down the pit and out back into the stream.'

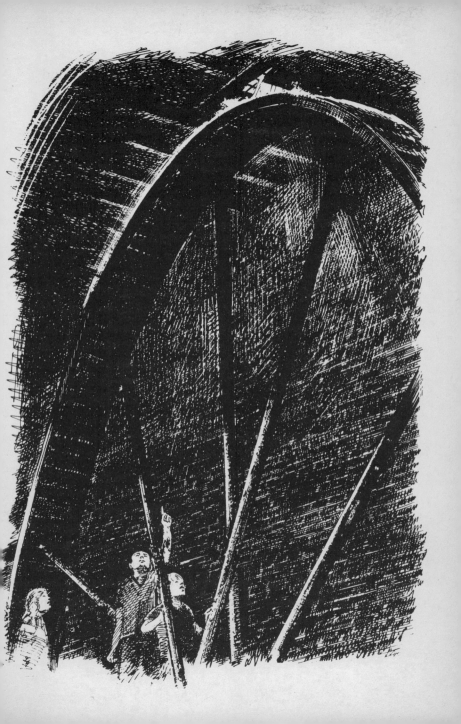

Sandra was practical.

'There's a lot of rubbish down there in the pit. We'll have to shift that.'

'Don't know,' called Ranji. He sprang like a cat on to the iron spokes. It gave a sudden grunt like a pig and the wheel lurched an inch or two. Before Sandra could move, Andy had jumped on. The wheel shot forward another foot then jerked to a stop, throwing Ranji and Andy back on to the rail. They picked themselves up, looking stupid.

'Pinbrains,' said Sandra.

'Hey,' I said. 'Don't let's fall out. We're nearly there. Let's break for lunch. Then we can split up. Two can lift out this muck and two can shift the junk from the gear pit next door.'

It was easier said than done. Clearing the wheel pit, which was mostly sticks and leaves and mud, took us all that day and the next. And when it came to shifting the gear wheels, it wasn't on. We pulled one or two to one side, all heaving on a rope we'd tied round. Some of the lighter bits we pulled clear from the gear pit and piled up to one side. After three days, we had to give up.

'We'll just have to hope it's all loose enough round that shaft for the wheel to turn,' said Ranji.

Hope. That was it. We were full of it. And why not?

That afternoon when we went home the water in the pool was quarter way up the planks we'd put in the sluice gate and was near the edge of the stone channel leading to the chute.

'Hey, we don't want it running over while we're away.'

'Right.'

We found a short plank and fixed it firmly across the mouth of the channel.

'It'll be forced to come up another foot before it gets over,' said Sandra.

Feeling terrific we cycled back into town early that evening. As we rode down the main street, Sandra turned to me and called,

'Hey, Mike, wasn't that your mate Steven?'

'Where? I didn't see him.'

'No, he wasn't looking at us, either. Seemed in a hurry.'

'You sure?'

'Sure, I'm sure. He was coming out of the library.'

Ranji laughed: 'Taylor? That'll be the day.'

16

Locked In

Next day was Saturday. The only way I knew one day from another on holiday, was that Mum was home after breakfast. I was all ready in my mill gear, tee shirt and jeans, and was stowing my bacon sandwiches in a plastic bag when she came into the kitchen.

'You, Mike. Are you going out all day today?'

Something in her voice worried me.

'Yeah, 'course I am, Mum.'

Sis stood in the doorway, in her dressing gown, yawning.

'Don't keep the great rambler from his beloved moors. He's the King of Penfold Forest, you know.'

Mum shook her head.

'I'd rather you didn't go out so far, Mike.'

She pointed to the window.

'Have you seen the sky?'

I had, and I'd been keeping quiet about it. It

had dawned grey. At least I think it had. But instead of clearing, white, then blue, it was turning a kind of orangey purple at the edges. And even at that time in the morning it was still and hot.

'Aw, Mum, I'll be all right.' I was desperate in case something stopped me from getting up to the secret mill today. Today was the big day. W for waterwheel day.

Mum hesitated. Sis joined in.

'Come on, Mum. A bit of rain won't do him any harm. He'll smell better. And as for getting struck by lightning . . .'

'Oh, all right. But is there somewhere where you can shelter?'

'Course there is Mum, there's . . .' then I stopped. I was so eager I had nearly given the secret away. Without waiting for any more argument or any helpful comments from Sis, I dashed out.

It was a bike day and it was hard work. The road to Penfold's mostly uphill once you're out of town. And the air was like an oven. The heat came at you off the road and little mirage pools formed at the top of every rise. We were streaming with sweat before we were even half way there.

And, guess what? Andy and Sandra were at war with one another. Was I glad when we finally struggled up the ridge and saw the valley. The sky by now was like a great dark lid over the moors and from far away you could hear the first growls

of thunder.

Andy threw his bike down and panted. The mill pool had filled up more and backed up covering some of the reed and grass clumps.

'Hey, come on, let's pull that plank out. I want to see that water run.'

But Sandra had him by the sleeve.

'No way, Andy. You wait. First we see everything is OK. Then we do it properly, and we do it all together.'

He looked violent for a moment. Then he calmed down. We trundled down the hill with our bikes. Ranji and I had our tee shirts off and tied round our waists. The sweat was running down my chest. I was getting sunburnt after these weeks up here. I looked at Ranji.

'Hey, you don't get a tan, do you? You've got one permanent.'

He laughed. 'That's what you think. If I get lots of sun I get deeper brown.'

'You're putting me on.'

He shook his head. 'It's skin same as yours. It just starts brown that's all.'

That was true. We grinned at one another and started to race the rest of the way.

We all four rushed in a big scramble into the mill yard just as the first lightning flash made a jagged streak across the skyline. We'd hardly got our bikes inside the mill when thunder crashed overhead. From inside it made a terrific bang.

'Hey, that's getting closer,' said Sandra.

'It's going to throw it down,' crowed Andy. 'Come on, let's get that launder opened. Then we can all be down here when the big rush comes.'

'Will you give over, our Andy.' Sandra's voice was high pitched now. Ranji and I looked at one another. She and her brother were building up for a real big one.

'It's the weather,' he laughed. 'We'll all feel better when it rains.'

'Come on,' I said. 'Let's go in the wheelhouse first and check the wheel's free – before we bring the water down.'

We dumped our gear and ran out round the side of the mill. As we did, a great burst of lightning spread like glass breaking all over the sky. Then came a tremendous roll of thunder and the heavens opened.

I felt the first drops on my bare skin. It was like a warm shower bath. Next moment the rain was sheeting down. Yelling and dancing as the water sluiced over our skin, we charged round the corner and pushed in through the gap.

'Hey, watch that wood block,' gasped Sandra as we ducked through. 'You knock that out and we'll be in trouble.'

We all pushed and shoved inside. It was strange and silent. The battering of the rain and the racket of the thunder seemed fainter, more far away. We could hear something else, though. The sound of water running through the open space at the end of the grid in the roof.

'Hey,' Andy was excited. 'It's running through already.'

'You wally,' said his sister. 'That's just rain coming down.'

'Wally yourself,' retorted Andy.

'Please, please,' put in Ranji. 'Let's not have private fights.'

He clambered up on to the iron spokes of the wheel and held up his hand, speaking pompously.

'Ladies and gentlemen. If I may make a few choice remarks on this suspicious occasion.'

'Boo, chuck him out, pay him off . .' we shouted.

Worked up now, Andy threw himself on to the

wheel and climbed up beside Ranji. As he did, the wheel gave a crack like a gun and swung down so suddenly that both of them were flung off against the rail. Ranji jumped clear but Sandra had to snatch Andy away before the paddles pulled him down into the side of the pit.

All her bottled up fury now burst out.

'You stupid little git!'

She shook him like a doll, big lump as he was. He grappled with her. It took all our strength to pull them apart. Her face was flushed, her eyes alight.

'I've had enough of you. Why should I be lumbered with a great thick onk who can't put one foot in front of another without tripping up . . .'

'And why should I be lumbered with a bossy cow of a sister!' screamed Andy.

The wheelhouse was suddenly quiet. I could hear the rain sluicing down the wall at the end and the splash as it landed in the bottom of the pit. Another incredible flash of lightning lit up the inside and I could see everyone's face, eyes staring.

Then, Andy said, between his teeth,

'Just for once, I am going to do what I want. I am going up there and I am going to take that plank out and don't you try and stop me.'

Sandra made a lunge for him. But he was gone. Two quick strides and he was at the gap in the door, fending off his sister as she charged after him. Half turned, he blundered out, forgetting to duck as he went. His head and shoulders struck the wedge in the door.

With a grumbling sound, the iron and wood folded inwards as the wood block tumbled down at our feet. And from outside came a grinding sound, then the clatter and crunch of falling bricks and stones as the stack gave way.

Sandra threw herself at the door.

'You, Andy, come back,' she yelled, as she struck against the iron surface. She turned and looked at us, her face dead pale in the gloom.

'Hey, I can't budge it. It's jammed.'

When the Wheel Stopped

Ranji and I pushed into the doorway beside Sandra and shoved with all our might. A great shock of pain ran from my shoulder down my arm and made me feel sick for a moment. But it made no difference. The bricks, tumbling down outside, had jammed the way out completely.

'Andy,' shouted Sandra, again. 'You come back and pull these bricks away.'

There was no answer. Just another clap of thunder, then the click and thud of a single brick falling, and after that the sound of the rain coming down.

'We're trapped,' she said. 'The little sod's gone off and left us.'

'No, San,' said Ranji, reasonably. 'He's probably scared stiff at what he's done and he's just run away. He'll come back.'

She shook her head. There were tears in her eyes

now.

'I have really had enough with him. I've had to look after him for five flaming years, now. Dad doesn't understand. He just thinks I ought to do it whether I like it or not.'

Ranji put his hand on her shoulder.

'I think, maybe, he'd be better off being on his own a bit. And so would you.'

'But Dad reckons he'll just get into trouble on his own. He *does* get into trouble.'

Ranji shrugged.

'He couldn't get into more trouble than he has today. And there are three of us looking after him.'

Sandra laughed. It was a shaky laugh.

'You're right. Trouble is, I get the blame.'

'Anyway, San,' I said. 'When he starts our school, your Dad'll just have to let him look after himself.' I thought a bit. 'He'll just *have* to look after himself.'

'Don't you worry. Little brother'll look after himself.' She made a face. 'Anyway, let's see about getting out of here.'

She crouched down and peered into the wheel pit.

'Can we crawl out through the shaft hole?'

I shook my head.

'No way. Think if the wheel started moving. You'd get minced. Anyway, there's not room and it's part blocked on the other side.'

'That wheel isn't going to turn,' answered

Sandra fiercely. 'Look, I've had enough of this place. Once we get out, it's straight home and forget it. Andy can go play with his stunt bike and I'll get back to my running.'

'Come on,' I said. 'After all this work we've done. We are going to see this wheel go round. Hey, maybe Andy's gone to get some help.'

'Not him. He's gone to take that plank out. He's got a one track mind.'

Ranji pointed upwards. 'I'm going up there. Perhaps I can squeeze out where the water comes down. I'm thinner than you two.'

'Ha ha. But you're not that thin.'

Ranji smiled and swung up on to the rail. But as he did, there was a sudden grinding, squealing noise, a harsh scraping that went right through to the roots of my teeth. Ranji jerked his leg back on to the rail, just in time as the wheel began to turn.

'It's moving on its own,' he shouted. Then his voice vanished as the whole wheelhouse began to shake with the rumble of the turning wheel and the air filled with spray as water poured out of the launder above and sluiced down the end wall.

The noise was horrible. It was unbelievable. It drowned out the thunder. You couldn't speak – it hurt even to open your mouth. And, if you spoke, you couldn't hear your own voice.

We grabbed and held on to each other as the brickwork rocked beneath us. I looked at Sandra. I could tell what she was thinking. That crazy brother of hers had pulled out the plank and let the water out of the pool. Her mouth opened, but I just shook my head. It was no good talking. We just had to hang on until someone came. It wasn't possible any more to try crawling out, either along the shaft or up the wheelhouse wall.

We were trapped, trapped until someone came. But who? And when? What time was it, I wondered as the bellowing of the wheel went through my head and made my ear drums quiver and pop. Lunch time, maybe. It would be hours before the family started looking for us. And even if Andy did the sensible thing – some hope – it could be hours before he found someone out on the Penfold Road, in this downpour.

Ranji punched me on the arm. He pointed to the slot in the roof where the water poured down. Through the sheet of water, light was streaming. Putting his mouth to my ear he yelled,

'Rain's stopping.'

'Big deal,' I yelled back. 'There's a tankful up the hill, and this could run for days.'

He jerked his head away with a pained look.

'What are you shouting for?'

What for? Because of the noise, that's what. Then I realised the noise wasn't there any more. The shrieking rumbling battering our ears had stopped.

'The wheel's not moving any more.'

Ranji grabbed Sandra's arm: 'Hey, your kid

74

must have blocked off the launder again.'

'No such luck.'

Sandra shook her head and pointed upwards. Now that the wheel was still, we could hear the steady low roar of water running down the launder channel overhead and plunging down, splashing and spraying over the paddles into the pit below.

'Well, at least we won't go deaf while we're here.' I was surprised how quiet my voice had gone. And how the sound echoed off the dank walls.

It was a little while later, we noticed that the sound of the pouring water had changed. There was a deeper note, duller, of water on water.

A flash of sunlight from the top of the wall brought a gleam back from below. Ranji stared at me. Then he turned to bend over the rail and peer into the pit. His face seemed to have gone grey.

'Mike, Sandra. The pit's filling up. That last lot of rubbish we left down there must have blocked the outlet.'

He paused, then went on in a whisper,

'This place is going to flood.'

18

Flood Water Peril

We stood in dead silence by the rail, watching the water in the pit. The bottom paddles of the wheel had vanished under the dark surface. Here and there were sparkling spots of light where the sun came through the vent at the top. Outside, the storm had blown over. No more thunder, no more lightning. Just the sound of the water running and the splash, splash of the pool below filling up.

Sandra spoke. Her voice was shaky.

'It'll be six o'clock before they start panicking at home. Another hour before they can get here.'

'Yeah – if they know where we are,' I said. My knuckles had gone numb and white where I was gripping the rail.

'They'll work it out,' Ranji spoke quickly. 'They're forced to.' But he was guessing. So were we all.

'Tell you what, San.' I turned to her. 'Your kid's

bound to meet someone on the top road. He can flag somebody down. He's bound to. He's not daft.'

'Not daft. Don't talk to me about our kid. Wish we'd come without him.'

'Ah, come on. He's no worse than other juniors,' I said. Ranji nodded.

'OK for you two to talk. You don't have to act mother half the time. Our Dad can't see.'

'Hey,' said Ranji, grabbing us both. 'We're stupid. We've forgotten that shaft hole, through the wall over there. When the water gets up that far, it'll run off. We get our feet wet, maybe. That's all.'

We didn't know whether to believe him or not, but we had no choice.

We settled down to wait. We sat close together on the rail. Inside the wheelhouse, the air was chill and getting chillier as the black water below crept up.

'Wish I hadn't left my sweater in the mill,' said Ranji, shivering.

We moved in even closer. Sandra found an old pencil stub in her pocket and we played noughts and crosses on our hands and arms, till the point went. We shifted about, climbed down, walked up and down flapping our arms.

I realised my stomach was empty. We hadn't eaten since breakfast and our sandwiches were with our bikes in the mill. We climbed back on the rail and leant against each other. The running water was monotonous. It had a funny effect, as though we weren't there any more. We were somewhere where time didn't count.

My head jerked up. Sandra's face was on my shoulder. Her eyes were closed. Ranji was leaning on her from the other side. He'd gone off too. I tried to keep time by counting. I didn't want to watch that water creeping up. I counted to 60 – to 300. That was five minutes. Thirty-six thousand made an hour. . . My mind wandered. I was at home. Dad was outside at the back, cleaning up the Dormobile. We were going off to Rhyl, lying in the sun, swimming in the sea.

Then I woke. My feet were freezing. I was up to my knees in cold, oily water. It had run over the edge of the pit and up the brick platform. The shaft hole wasn't drawing it off fast enough. This place was like a bottle, filling up – and we were inside.

'Wake up, wake up!' I shook them. Their eyes opened, alarmed.

We all scrambled up on to the rail, and struggled up among the iron spokes of the great wheel. Now we had to hang on.

Time passed. The light at the top seemed to dim as if the sun had clouded over. More rain? Oh no! We shifted up another spoke as the water caught at our feet again. It was moving faster now, I was sure.

My head started to spin. I was dizzy with hunger. Earlier I had been seeing things, dreaming. . . Now I was hearing things. The bumping

78

rattle and roar of a lorry engine. Someone shouting. I looked at Sandra and Ranji. They had their arms and legs hooked round the spoke, their heads on their chests. Asleep. I *was* hearing things.

There was silence again. My eyes went blank inside my eyelids. I was going to faint and fall off into the pit.

Suddenly it came again. Closer. A man's voice shouting.

'Get up that hill and open the sluice, for a start, so the water'll run off down the stream. And you come and help me round t'other side.'

'Sandra, Ranji,' I nudged them.

They woke and stared wildly at me.

'There's somebody outside.'

'You're dreaming.'

'No, listen.'

From close outside came the rattle, crunch and click as bricks were pulled up and flung aside. Then a wrench as someone heaved at the door.

'Look out,' shouted Ranji. 'This place is half full of water.'

The door was jerked back. Light flooded in from outside. Filthy water surged out in a great wave through the gap and across the ground outside. Someone swore, violently, three times.

We scrambled down and waded out into the fresh air, breathing it in as if it cost ten quid a time. Then we stared.

Facing us were three people. One was a tall,

lean, black-haired man in singlet and jeans. The others we knew.

One was Spotty Sam Taylor, grinning all over his ugly mug. And Steve was next to him. How did they get up here? And beyond them, by the bushes on the bank of the stream, suddenly appeared Andy. He'd been crying. His face was smudged. His clothes were soaking. But now he was laughing with relief.

19

Rescued – but . . .

Andy leapt at his sister and grabbed her.

'I didn't pull that plank out! It were running over the top. The pond was flooded. I tried to get the planks loose from the sluice, but they wouldn't budge. So I ran all the way up to the main road and miles down it. I couldn't find anybody.'

I could see relief on Sandra's face as she hugged her kid brother. It was him who'd shut us in, but it was him who'd saved us. She turned to the man, then hesitated.

Spotty Sam smirked in that stupid way he always does when he sees Sandra.

'This is our Uncle Bill. We were coming up Penfold road, when we saw your kid running along screaming.'

'I weren't screaming,' protested Andy. 'I was shouting.'

Sandra turned to Sam's uncle.

'We have to thank you, then. It could have been hours before our families came looking for us. It was a spot of real luck, you were coming by on the main road.'

'Oh, it weren't luck, Sandra,' said Sam, getting familiar. 'We were coming here anyway. Our kid found out about this place with a load of old gear in it, so we came up to collect it.'

Ranji and I looked at Steve. He stared back, then looked away. Sam's uncle jerked his thumb towards the mill, then set off round the corner of the wheelhouse, calling over his shoulder,

'Don't hang about, then. We want that lot loaded up before dark.'

We looked at each other, then followed Spotty Sam and Steve, who'd run off after their uncle. In the mill yard stood the old scrappie truck, tail gate down. It was backed up to the open double doors.

Ranji raced ahead and stood in the doorway, blocking it.

'You're not taking all those gear irons.'

Sam's uncle stared.

' 'Course we are, Snowball. That's how we earn us living.'

He turned to Sam.

'There's too much here for one load. We'll take that smaller stuff stacked up by the pit.'

Ranji exploded. 'But we pulled all that out.'

'You did what? That must have taken you weeks.'

Sam's uncle was laughing.

'What did you do that for?'

'We were getting the mill going. You've got no right to smash it up for scrap. It's not yours.'

'And it's not yours, Snowball.'

Sam's uncle pushed past Ranji and disappeared into the half dark inside of the mill building. We all followed, wondering what to do. Inside I could tell the floor had started to flood. Our bikes were lying in inches of water, our lunch packs, sweaters, the lot, were sopping wet. But Ranji didn't seem to care. He stood against the lorry tail gate, where it was ranged across the open doorway, as if he wanted to stop them moving the iron by force.

Sam's uncle picked up the nearest of the pile of metal wheels and leaning past Ranji, slung it with a great crash into the back of the lorry.

'Look,' he said, as he turned back for more. 'If the council or somebody else wants to tart up this place, they're welcome, though God knows why they should. Waste of money. Well, if they do, they can have all this gear from us. We'll look after it. They'll just have to pay handling and transport charges.'

He laughed. Sam joined in. Steve was just starting to smile, when they both saw Sandra and Ranji looking at them and changed their minds.

'Am I the only one working round here?' demanded Sam's uncle. 'Get grafting, you two.'

He looked at us.

'We'll give you a lift down to town if you like. And you can show willing by helping load up, eh?'

Sandra shook her head. She was just as angry as Ranji, but she was calmer.

'No, thanks, Mr Taylor. We've got us bikes. We're – very grateful to you for getting us out of there,' she pointed to the wheelhouse. 'But we put a lot of work into siding this mill and we don't think you've any right to take the gear.'

Sam's uncle heaved another load of iron on to the truck. It was half full now.

'Look. Never mind about rights. You just get off home then and forget about us. You be grateful we came up here and we'll be grateful you didn't see us taking this gear out.'

Sandra picked up her bike and other stuff and was wheeling it out to the doorway. Andy did the same. I was going to pick up mine when I noticed that Ranji wasn't there any more. He'd vanished.

But next minute we all saw where he was. There was a humming, gritty noise from the cab of the old truck. We all stared in amazement as the back suddenly began to lift in the air.

Sam's uncle swore and rushed alongside the truck. But he was too late. The whole load of iron rods and cogs was sliding and crashing into a heap on to the water-logged floor of the old mill.

20

Ranji in Danger

It was so silent in the old mill, I could hear the faint trickle of water still running down the launder. Outside, the sun was going down over the moors and now it shone straight in through the gap in the doorway. There we stood, Sandra and Andy and me with our bikes on one side of the opening – Sam and Steve on the other.

Sam's uncle snatched open the cab door, dragged Ranji out and threw him down on to the floor behind the tangled heap of scrap metal.

'Right, Snowball. You can't leave well alone. You're going to find out what happens to people like you.'

Sandra spoke.

'Leave him alone.'

He turned.

'And you can shut your gob. I should have left you lot in there to cool off till we got this stuff away. I want my head seeing to.'

Ranji staggered to his feet. His face was bleeding from a cut. But his eyes were full of anger, no trace of fear, as he turned from one to another.

'You load it up, I'll tip it out again.'

'Wrong, Snowball. You and your mates are going to load it up. But first of all . . .'

He looked round the space behind the doors and then picked up a long piece of wood.

'First of all, you are going to get a thrashing. Just so we don't have a next time.'

He gripped Ranji's arm. I could see the pain in Ranji's face. Then he held out the stick to Steve.

'OK, kid. You first. Give him half a dozen. Then you, Sam.'

My eye caught Steve's. We looked at one another. Then he shook his head.

'Nah, forget it.'

Now the stick was held out to Sam. But he had his eyes on Sandra. She wasn't saying anything, but Sam knew what she was thinking. He shook his head.

'Nah. Let's leave it. Let 'em go. It's more trouble than it's worth. Anyway, there's no guarantee we'll get this lot back up the hill. The old truck won't take it.'

'Right.' Sam's uncle spoke through clenched teeth. 'Do I have to do everything myself?'

He forced Ranji's arm up his back and bent him over. The stick rose in the air. I could see Sandra getting ready to jump. I braced myself.

But right at that moment, someone spoke from the gap in the doorway beside the truck.

'Mister, leave that boy alone, if you please.'

21

Who's for the Hammer?

In the doorway, tall and thin, dark against the setting sun, was Ranji's father. He stepped out from behind the edge of the tailgate.

'Leave that boy alone.'

Sam's uncle lowered the stick, but did not let go of Ranji's arm.

'What do you want?' he demanded.

'That is my son and I do not allow anyone to touch him.'

'And what are you going to do about it?'

Sam's uncle's eyes were screwed up against the sun shining through the doorway. His mouth was thin.

Ranji's Dad bent down by the wheel of the truck. When he stood up, I saw he had in his hand one of the sledge hammers scrappies carry. He swung it lightly and I realised those thin arms must be strong.

'Let my son go, or I will knock you into the ground like a tent peg.'

Something came up in my throat, half a laugh, half a gulp.

But Sam's uncle did not think it was funny. And he was looking not at Ranji's Dad, but behind him. He let Ranji go. Ranji straightened up rubbing his arm. Then someone else came past the truck and stood there.

'Hey, Dad,' I gasped. Behind him was our Sis.

Seeing her seemed to make up Sam's uncle's mind for him. He nodded to Steve and Sam.

'Get in the cab.'

'What about the gear?' asked Sam, a baffled look on his face.

'—— the gear', was the short, sweet reply. 'Get in.'

He turned to Ranji's Dad. I was sure he was going to say something. But then he remembered there were witnesses and he said no more.

The truck engine gasped, coughed, then roared away. A huge puff of purple smoke filled the space and set us all choking. Then with a grind of gears it pulled out and bumped away over the yard. There was silence again, save for the trickle of water from the wheelhouse.

Dad turned to us.

'Right, you lot. Let's go home. You can tell us the story on the way. It'll need to be good.'

22

Let's Go Home

The Dormobile was parked just down the Penfold road. By the time we had got there, stowed the bikes on the rack and piled in, it was getting dark. Dad started the engine, switched on the headlights and we rolled off on the road to home.

When Sandra had done telling the story of how we'd found the mill and got the wheel going again, we were half way there.

Dad shook his head: 'Well, I reckon you can give industrial archeology a rest for the holidays.'

'Hey but Dad,' I said, 'what if the Taylors come back and nick all that scrap?'

He changed down as we went up another rise. The town lights were showing across the moors.

'I don't think they'll touch that now. It's too much trouble, and Bill Taylor's enough problems with the law as it is.'

He turned to Ranji's Dad.

'I'm more concerned about you and Ranji.'

Ranji's Dad smiled thinly.

'If I were worrying about people like Taylor all the time I would give up the ghost. You show them you're frightened and they trample all over you.'

Dad nodded. There was silence for a while, then I got my question in.

'Hey Dad, how did you get here so soon? How did you find out?'

Sis laughed. She was at the back with her arms round Sandra and Andy. He was asleep already.

'Well, our Mam thought something was wrong when you didn't come home after the storm. So we went round to Ranji's house to see if they knew where you were. But in the end you can thank your little friend Steven. We knew you were up Penfold Forest way, but where? Then I remembered Steven had come into the reference library and asked if he could see the same book you'd been looking at –'

'Hey, yes. But how did you know exactly where?' I asked.

'Well, there was this toffee paper stuck in the page as a marker. Old habits die hard.'

There was a big laugh. Then Sandra started to sing and we sang all the way down the hill into town. When we got to,

'Ilkley Moor b'aht 'at,'

I saw Ranji's Dad was joining in.

Before I could stop myself, I asked,

92

'Where did you learn that?'

He smiled.

'My father was with the British Army in the Punjab. He learnt a lot of songs. Some I cannot repeat.'

'I bet,' said Sis.

We swung round the corner of the street where Sandra and Andy lived. I noticed then, for the first time, that Ranji hadn't said a word. He was sitting at the side, a quiet smile on his face.

In next to no time we were home.

23

Sorting Things Out

Well, did our gang break up, after all? Well, it did and it didn't.

We didn't go back to the mill. People are working on it now, restoring it. They don't seem to want our expert advice.

Sandra went back to her running. She'll be representing the club next year. And her Dad's seen sense and let her transfer from St Winifred's to our school. That saves a lot of hassle.

And Andy? I saw him the other day on the Rec with his bike and the usual bunch of smaller kids tagging along. He's a big wheel, if you know what I mean. He's in the first year at our school.

We'll all be there now, but different years, different worlds.

And Steve? I haven't seen him much. That'll have to wait. I'm in two minds about it.

But when I asked Ranji what he thought, he just laughed.

'Oh that, Mike. Just water over the mill, that is.'

CHALLENGE IN THE DARK

Robert Leeson

Mike Baxter's first day at his new school marks the start of an unforgettable and challenging week – not least when he makes an enemy of Steven Taylor and his bullying older brother, Spotty Sam. Mike's friends 'help out' by setting up a dare for both him and his enemy Steven Taylor – to stay in an old disused underground shelter. Before either has much time to protest they find themselves exposed to real dangers, experiencing fear and panic as a result of more than playground victimization.

'This short adventure has the same unmistakable veracity and friendly humour that has made *The Demon Bike Rider* so popular with young readers.' *Growing Point*

The Demon Bike Rider by Robert Leeson is also in Lions.